Copyright © 2022 by Lor Gislason
Cover Art © 2022 by Eduardo Valdés-Hevia
Interior Illustration © Matt Pierce
Interior Illustration © Enoch Duncan
Interior Illustration © Kelly Coleman
Interior Illustration © Dood
Interior Illustration © Trevor Henderson
Interior Illustration © Jonathan La Mantia
Interior Illustration © SJ Miller

First published in 2022 by DarkLit Press

ISBN 978-1-7386585-2-7 (Paperback)
ISBN 978-1-7386585-5-8 (Ebook)

Praise for Inside Out

Inside Out is a heart-pounding, brain-melting, stomach-turning phenomenal debut from Lor Gislason, that serves a fresh and oozing take on traditional body-horror. Entwined amongst the gloop, gore and gaping wounds, lies a powerful tale of what it means to be human, in whatever form that takes. Visceral and spectacular.

- Tabatha Wood, author of *Seeds*

"Lor Gislason's Inside Out turns body horror, well, inside out. In the wake of a contagion that melts and mutates flesh, Gislason stitches together flash fiction vignettes from over a dozen points of view, scooping out the plague's messy physical, emotional, and even spiritual ramifications on the survivors. Fast-paced and insightful, while never less than gleefully and deliriously gruesome, Inside Out is a squirming treat for horror fans. "

- Gordon B. White, author of *Rookfield*

"Inside Out's series of vignettes from the front lines of a horrific pandemic is prescient, heartfelt, and disgustingly entertaining. It is goopy and visceral, but those things don't matter without heart. Lor makes us care about their characters quickly, in a way that had me dreading what would come next. Ultimately, Inside Out is about all of us, about moving on with normalcy in the face of horrendously abnormal circumstances, the consequences of willful ignorance and hubris, and the danger and necessity of hope. It's also just ridiculously bonkers fun. This is easily one of my favourite pieces of pandemic horror fiction in the last few years."

- Brandon Applegate, author of *Those We Left Behind and Other Sacrifices*

"Gislason takes us on a disgustingly fun, flexible romp through weird science and nightmare biology. Inside Out is an exciting and surprising journey through a wanton world of goop."

- Joe Koch, author of *The Wingspan of Severed Hands*

Inside Out is a kaleidoscope of goop and gore and I couldn't read it quick enough. It's like Gislason took *The Blob* and *Society* and everything that ever melted and gathered it all up into one big squirming, pulsating, bubble of goo. I loved it.

- Luke Kondor, author of *The Run Fantastic*, Showrunner for The Other Stories podcast

"A fascinating mosaic of human experiences, each leading us deep through a gauntlet of the bodily macabre."

- Hailey Piper, author of *Queen of Teeth*

INSIDE OUT

Lor Gislason

DARKLIT
PRESS

Content Warning

The story that follows may contain
graphic violence and gore.

Please go to the very back of the book
for more detailed content warnings.

Beware of spoilers.

In Memory of C.

Contents

SEGMENT 1 - THE INCIDENT   1

SEGMENT 2 - THE FAMILY   5

SEGMENT 3 - THE INSTITUTE   11

SEGMENT 4 - THE EXPLODING MAN   15

SEGMENT 5 - THE CHILD   17

SEGMENT 6 - THE LANDLORD   23

SEGMENT 7 - THE VIRGIN   27

SEGMENT 8 - THE ZIT   33

SEGMENT 9 - THE PATROL   39

SEGMENT 10 - THE TATTOOIST   45

SEGMENT 11 - DAILY BRIEFING, APRIL 25th   53

SEGMENT 12 - THE PILE   55

SEGMENT 13 - THE PRIEST   61

SEGMENT 14 - THE SCIENTIST   64

SEGMENT 15 - THE NON-BELIEVER   71

FINAL SEGMENT – REINTEGRATION   79

AFTERWORD   85

SEGMENT 1
THE INCIDENT

MUST HAVE CLEARANCE LEVEL 3 TO ACCESS.
REPORT TO SUPERIOR OFFICER BEFORE/AFTER
VIEWING.
ANY FAILURE TO RETURN DOCUMENTS WILL BE MET
WITH IMMEDIATE NJP.

FBC REPORT 74311 - INCIDENT ALPHA
[REDACTED] MINING FACILITY, BRITISH COLUMBIA,
CANADA
MARCH 14TH, 20XX

Team lead Daniel [REDACTED] received radio
transmission at approx. 1:35 A.M. from the pit crew
requesting medical personnel. Upon arriving at the scene,
EMT and security officers could not locate any of the
twelve-man crew. (SEE - PERSONNEL LIST) Equipment
was in a state of disarray, covered in blood and presumed
human tissue. Fragments of clothing were found in similar
conditions. Attached are photographs taken by Robin
[REDACTED - PRESUMED DECEASED] a member of the
on-site security team who went missing shortly after.
SEE LBC-1, LBC-2, LBC-3
      FBC operatives were on the scene in approx. 2 hours'
time. Clean-up and containment was successful. Senior FBC
staff remained to coordinate with the [REDACTED]
company. The official cause will be listed as a collapse due
to a landslide. Sole survivor: Daniel [REDACTED] was
brought in for questioning. Vitals were checked: elevated BP
and heart rate but otherwise within normal levels. Attached
is a transcript of his interview:

Harris: Hello, again, Daniel. We spoke not too long ago; do you remember me? I'm Agent Harris. I'd like to ask you a few questions. Do you go by Daniel, or do you prefer Dan?

Daniel: Daniel is fine... listen, I need to call my wife. S-she doesn't know where I am.

Harris: Don't worry, your family has been contacted and they are in a safe location.

Daniel: Oh! Oh. Good. I'd like to speak with her after this if I can.

Harris: We can certainly arrange that. Now, can you tell me a bit about what happened early this morning?

Daniel: I'm...not sure how much sense it will make.

Harris: That's all right. Take your time.

Daniel: (After approx. 1-minute silence) Jules called me over the radio a bit after 1 A.M. He sounded frantic, scared. He was screaming... I had to get him to slow down and repeat himself, couldn't understand a lick of what he was saying. Has a heavy Newfie accent, sounds like gibberish at the best of times. He said--said people were eating each other. I assumed he had fallen asleep and had a nightmare. It's not uncommon for night shift to take naps here and there when things get slow. Not a big deal if everything's done on time. So, I asked him, 'you want me to send somebody?' He yells, 'Yes, yes, get over here right now'.

So, me, a four-man EMT crew, and a couple of security guy's head down there. Lighting plant had been knocked over, making it hard to see. Nobody around. We started calling out and got no response. Walk over to where Jules and them were digging–they must have hit a cave, there was a huge open hole. I was worried they may be trapped. Terry shined his flashlight around and it was just. Red. Walls, floor, ceiling...mineral deposit, you know how that stuff changes once it hits the open air? Then the smell hit us.

Harris: Can you describe this smell?

2

Daniel: It was sweet, but not in a good way. Like burnt sugar. Or garbage. We wear masks to prevent dust exposure, you know, things like that. I could smell it clear as day even through my mask. Made my throat scratchy. I think one of the guys ran off to throw up.

We go into the cave…and I see the red stuff is fuzzy, like moss or mould, and it's covering everything. I pushed some of it around with my boot and it moved, like a vibration travelling outwards. One of the security guys…Gordon? Gary? He tells us to come over. He's standing over a bunch of clothes and more fuzz. Some of it…it looked like organs. Oh, my God. I think that was them. Jules… (Muffled sobs are heard)

Harris: Daniel, it's OK. We are here to help you. So, you found no survivors?

Daniel: (after several minutes) No. There was no one.

Further questions were met with slurred speech and confusion.

After the investigation concluded, the mining site was shut down permanently. Incident Beta occurred in Peru approx. 36 hours later. Daniel (hereafter referred to as Subject 0) was transported to a secure FBC isolation facility. His body began to decompose in a matter of hours. Tissue samples, medical history and A/V recordings are available upon request. SEE FILES MMBC-A THROUGH S3.

SEGMENT 2
THE FAMILY

Julie was in the deepest part of her dream when she woke from someone nudging her. "Hmm?!" she sounded more annoyed than she was.

"Mom, there's a man outside. He smells bad."

All the hair on Julie's neck stood up. "Okay, sweetie, I'll go check it out. You wait here with Daddy, okay?" Kristy nodded, rubbing the sleep from her eyes. The shy seven-year-old was a fairly light sleeper and had frequent nightmares. Julie assumed it was one of those, but something about the way she said he smells bad set her on edge. Kristy had never said something like that about a dream before.

After setting her down next to Steve, who was sleeping like a log and snoring like always, Julie went to the kitchen to get a flashlight. The house was quiet, the only noise was the tick-ticking of the clock above the cupboards. It had been a good week, overall, but she was looking forward to going back to sleep after she set Kristy's mind at ease. It was all part of being a mom, after all.

Rounding the corner towards the front door, Julie paused. Wait. I do smell something. What is that? Her face scrunched up as she got closer. Flicking on the flashlight, Julie's eyes went wide as she saw the distinct shape of a person outside the door. It was too dark to see anything more than that. The porch light was off, too. There was something strange about the shape. Moving back and forth to see it better through the glass pane, she approached the door. Locked. Thank God.

Thump. Julie nearly jumped out of her skin. Was it knocking?

"Hello?" she said nervously. "Is someone there? Can I help you?"

"Hhhhhhhhppppbbrr.." Thump. Thump.

Okay. That was clearly knocking. Is there a drunk dude outside my door? "W-we have a gun in the house! Please go away. I will call the police!" Fuck, why did I ask him please? She stood to the side of the door, trying to get a better look at the man. She was pretty sure it was a man. Large frame, low voice.

"Youpppbbbb aaannnffff MEeee….SOOoo HAaaaappppbbbb Togaaaaatheeeoooopp"

Singing. Definitely drunk. That smell was intense, with only the door separating them. Julie was nearly gagging, her hand covering her face. It was hot, tangy. She began to turn around intending to go back to the kitchen and grab the phone. Or wake Steve. Or both.

WHAM! Julie jumped, unable to stop a tiny shriek from escaping. She whipped around to face the door again and nearly let out another noise. The man had slapped his arm on the door, but it was unlike any arm she'd ever seen. Sickly pink with brown splotches, pulsing like a giant vein. It slid down, leaving a sticky residue with streaks of matter on the glass, with a revolting sheeek noise. The smell somehow got worse. "Yoouuuuuupp aaaaaann. MEe.." the thing that was most assuredly not a man groaned. It sounded like it was dealing with a mouth full of spit, gurgling, coughing, struggling to get the words out.

Panic rose in Julie faster than she'd ever known. "STEVE! Steve, wake up. There's something outside!" She sprinted back into the bedroom, scooping up Kristy who was hugging a teddy bear to her chest. The shaking child was as light as a feather in her arms, as adrenaline was pumping steadily through her body. Steven sprang up, pulling on a discarded pair of jeans from the day before. She hurried through an explanation, and left him to hopefully deal with it, while she and Kristy retreated to the safety of the attic.

6

Steve got the shotgun out of the gun safe. He'd never had to use it and definitely didn't want to shoot a weird drunk leper. Julie had a tendency to exaggerate and he knew it wasn't that bad. But, as the man of the house, sometimes you have to settle the hen's worries. He'd just threaten to shoot them, turn them around, and settle back into bed. After all, he had work in the morning and needed his sleep.

Thump. Sheeeeeeek.

"What the fuck?" The front entrance smelled like rotten fish and shit smeared together. Steve covered his face with his arm and leaned the shotgun against the glass with the other, intending to show he meant business. He didn't want the rankest hobo alive standing outside his house a minute longer. "Hey man…You gotta go. I've got my gun here…" he tapped the barrel against glass. "I really don't want to use it."

Silence. Steve counted to ten and breathed a sigh of relief. Crisis averted.

THUMP. THUMP.

Colour drained from Steve's face. "Are you trying to break down my door you fucking asshole!?" he struggled to pull the few shells he brought with him out of his jeans pocket. Shitshitshitshit! Silence again and Steve glanced towards the door. The shape had retreated and behind it. In the light of the street, more were there. He turned on the porch light and instantly regretted it. Standing together were masses of pink and brown meat, swaying like wheat in a breeze. The one that came to his door (Steve assumed, but it was so hard to tell, they all looked so similar) had a hole where its face should be. Fluid leaked out of the cavity. A long tongue peeked out the side, a parody of human expression. Suddenly it fell, tumbling end over end out of the creature. As it dropped, it fell faster, with more and more still coming. Like a magician with endless, fleshy scarves. Finally, a mass fell out of it and onto the ground with a horrid

7

plop. Squinting, Steve leaned his face against the glass to get a better look at it. He retreated just as fast.

"Jesus Christ." It was a pile of human tongues, stuck together end to end. It lay in a snakelike coil. He fell back against the wall, hands shaking. The creature slammed into the doorframe again, making Steve jump. Another slam and the glass shattered, the mass flowing through the hole like water over rocks, undeterred by the sharp edges. Blood oozed freely from wounds sustained but they did not seem to bother the moving flesh.

Steve steadied himself, let out a puff of breath. He brought the stock down as hard as he could. Striking the creature again and again. It was as if he did nothing at all, for the creature did not flinch or slow down its movement. Steve yelled in frustration and struck a final time. This time, there was a response--the gun stuck in the body, removed from Steve's grip so suddenly he was caught off balance. It held strong and began silently sucking the firearm into itself. Then, it paused as if in thought before swinging the gun wildly, smashing more glass, and hitting the wall above where Steve had been standing moments earlier. A clatter and it released. Steve looked down and saw the thing that used to be his shotgun, now broken and twisted, the stock melted as if it was burnt plastic. It was still coming through, the distraction dealt with. Without a second thought, he ran.

Julie was pacing the small attic, from window to window. Kristy sat near her, crying and hiccuping. Steve moved frantically around the room, his eyes darting, thinking. "We have to get out, now," his voice hitched, giving away his emotions. "I don't know what the hell they are but there's a dozen out there." He abruptly stopped in front of the window and lifted the latch open. Looking back at Julie, his face set in stone.

"Where's the gun?" she asked.

"One of those...THINGS grabbed it from me and destroyed it like it was fucking nothing. This is...this is bad, Julie. Grab Kristy and get out there. I'm right behind you."

They could hear the things downstairs, the voice of a thousand whispers at once and splintering wood as they knocked over everything that came into contact with their flesh. Steve began piling boxes and old furniture in front of the attic door, glancing back at Julie. "We...we don't have the car keys." Her voice was barely audible. "What are we going to do?"

"We're going to run."

THE INSTITUTE

A TOWN IN SHOCK: MYSTERIOUS SUBSTANCE DUMPED BY INSTITUTE INTO LOCAL RIVER

Residents of [REDACTED] were left outraged tonight after photos of the prestigious Institute dumping "red liquid" into the Herring River. Several persons in Hazmat gear were seen emptying large barrels late at night, possibly to avoid detection. The [REDACTED] Chronicle received these photos from a concerned citizen who wishes to remain anonymous and fears for their safety.

"After I took the photos, I realized I was being watched," They recounted. "A company Jeep approached my car as I was leaving and tried to confiscate my camera. I had my phone out recording the whole thing."

Experts have attested to the validity of the recording and that it is NOT doctored. We reached out to the Institute for comment, their PR manager stated: "Our company develops pharmaceuticals that help save lives. These accusations are baseless and insulting. All members of the public with concerns can contact us at [EMAIL/PHONE] or visit our office during opening hours."

It is my job at the Chronicle to report the FACTS. The fact is that our community has been left out of discussions when it comes to The Institute for too long. I encourage everyone to join me at the next city council meeting where we are proposing a thorough investigation into these illegal practices and find out exactly what they're up to.

FRANK BRANDT, NEWS TEAM

"Absolute drivel." Reggie folded the newspaper and tossed it down on his desk. "Who the hell does he think he is? Asshole acts like he deserves a Pulitzer for sneaking around at night."

Alex looked over her glasses at Dr. Reggie Young before adjusting them silently. Best not to say anything. She continued tracking the live feed of specimens on her computer with mild interest, already feeling a headache starting.

"They should be thanking us," Reggie continued, his exasperation clear as day. "You think anything happens in this backwater town? A blueberry festival. That's it. We brought jobs and money, and this is how they repay us. We're just dumping greywater while the system fixed!!" He had a short fuse even on good days and once he got going, nothing would stop him. Alex was not surprised that Reggie remained a bachelor, even in his mid-50s. Heaven help the woman who becomes Mrs. Young.

With a whap, he slammed a hand on the desk, twisting to shake a finger in Alex's direction. "You know what I'm going to do?"

I couldn't give a rat's ass, she thought. "What?" she said.

Reggie had already sat down at his desk across from hers, their monitors back-to-back. "I'm going to get this dickhead fired." His chicken-pecked typing turned a budding annoyance into a full-blown migraine for Alex.

She pushed her chair out and stood up. "I'm gunna take an early lunch. You need me to get anything? I'll probably stop by Laurie's department on my way back." Alex's wife, who also worked at the Institute, was regarded as one of the best biologists in the field today. They often joked and addressed each other formally. "Dr. Forrester, could you pass the salt?" "Why certainly, Dr. Forrester." While they giggled, their son Samir would sink as low as possible into the couch, trying to disappear.

"Tell her to get her fucking act together before this PR fiasco turns into an even bigger shitstorm. And get me the dailies." He sounded like he was trying to murder his keyboard.

Alex found Laurie dissecting a specimen. She stood back and watched as she delicately sliced open muscle tissue with a surgical scalpel, peeling it away from her main quarry. Her forehead slightly creased in concentration. The acrid, burning smell made Alex's nostrils twinge. "I was going to offer you lunch," she said, peering over the operating table, "but I think I've lost my appetite."

"Oh, come on. It's not that bad." Laurie pulled off her gloves with a snap and smirked at her wife. "I can take a break from this one."

"What's it this week?" Sometimes Alex couldn't tell what the lumps of flesh used to be.

"Bear. We've had higher success rates with omnivores and the bigger, the better it seems. Here-" Laurie took a pair of forceps from her implement tray and moved the tissue around. "You can see the filaments have connected with the bear's stomach lining. The older parts are darker red, extending in a circular pattern like rings. It's begun to break down some of the muscles to reconfigure it."

"And that's why it smells sweet, yeah?"

"Yeah exactly. It's a by-product of the lichen breaking down the material around itself." As she poked and prodded, the muscle contracted. "That's just a reaction from the nervous system. We only work with dead tissue in here right now, as long as you don't touch it you should be fine."

As they spoke, Alex has leaned closer and closer to the lump of bear flesh. Now that the smell from the laser had dissipated, the sweetness of the moss was intoxicating. Her head pulsing from the migraine, she closed her eyes and took a deep breath to calm herself. The scent filled her thoughts and she pictured juicy strawberries, smothered in whipped cream atop a sponge cake. Without realizing it Alex started drooling. Laurie shook her arm.

"Hey, you in there? Did I go overboard again with the technical talk?" She stiffened. "Are you OK love?"

Alex opened her eyes. She reached down with both hands and touched the flesh as if it was a lover, savouring the way it felt, the softness under her hands, warm and wet. Slick tendrils snaked up her arms, wrapping tight. Laurie froze. The ropes retracted, slamming Alex on the metal table. Oblivious, she gazed blankly at her wife as her face was enveloped by the mass, the sweet odour now emanating from her liquefying flesh.

THE EXPLODING MAN

From: Deborah Townsend
Date: Wednesday 18 March 20XX 12.49pm
To: GTA Transit Support Desk
Subject: Incident on Barrie line - Monday, May 16

Hello,

I am writing concerning an incident I witnessed during the afternoon lull on the Barrie line, this last Monday (May 16th). I am an annual pass owner and expect compensation for the emotional trauma this has caused me!! I was returning from some shopping and boarded a train heading South. A man wearing ratty clothes, a black toque and dirty running shoes came up to me demanding change so I of course refused. He sat down across from me and started ranting and raving!! I was scared for my life. There was NO transit authority around and no other passengers helped me. I was about to call the cops myself when he stood up and vomited all over my pants! Then he proceeded to fall to the floor and pretend to have a fit. I cannot BELIEVE you would allow someone inebriated to travel. This is completely unacceptable. When we arrived at the next station I ran to the doors to find help and when I turned back the man was GONE and had left a pile of clothes and a huge mess!! There were FECES everywhere.

If I do not receive a full refund on my transit pass and money to cover dry cleaning, PLUS EXTRA I will be contacting the newspaper. YOU HAVE BEEN WARNED!!

-Deb

From: GTA Transit Support Desk
Date: Wednesday, 18 March 20XX 1.15pm
To: Deborah Townsend
Re: Incident on Barrie line - Monday, May 16

Hi Deborah,

We have looked into the incident you mention taking place
on the 16th of May. No man matching your description was
found in the area. However, we have had an influx of the
homeless sleeping on benches at the GTA stations. To
alleviate this problem, we have removed all benches. We
hope this helps!

Regards,
Brian

SEGMENT 5
THE CHILD

It had been a week since her parents died. Well, died was a strong term. They were still "here," generally speaking. Alice wasn't sure how much of her mom and dad were left in the Parent Thing. It certainly couldn't speak, or really interact with her at all. "Parent Thing" was what she called it in her head. Out loud, she didn't really call it anything.

She had come home from school that first day and went down to the basement (her dad loved to call it the "rumpus room," like it was a hip, new thing) and thought she caught them having sex--embarrassed, she hightailed it out of there while yelling at them to "get a room" and slammed several doors during her retreat. Hours later, slightly past dinner time, she called to them from the top of the stairs and got nothing. Feeling equal parts very embarrassed and very foolish for worrying, Alice braved opening the door and peeking down the stairs.

Her parents were in the same position as earlier. "Are you guys OK? Do you need me to call someone?" she had teased them. Her mom turned to look at her, and suddenly Alice was no longer joking. The face that once belonged to a kind, gentle woman was distorted beyond recognition. The skin was shiny and wet, as if covered in oil. Her eyes were gone. The space they once occupied was leaking a milky substance. The hair was still there, but it looked like a cheap wig barely clinging to the scalp. The worst part was her mouth. Well--their mouths. Mom and Dad were stuck together at the lips, skin that was once two people, now one. Hairs from her father's stubble mingled with smears of her mother's lipstick.

Alice screamed and slammed the door. She vomited until there was nothing left. Tried to go to sleep later that night and failed. When she used her phone, the results online were even worse--people becoming monsters just like her parents, cities setting up safe zones, looting and robberies happening constantly. Everything had gone to shit.

Well, at least I don't have to go to school, Alice thought bitterly.

After a few days, a routine began to settle in. Alice would sit at the top of the stairs in the afternoon and throw down meat from the freezer to her parents and chat with them. More like talk at them, since they couldn't talk back. Everyday, it got less human-looking and goopier. It reminded Alice of some of the videos they watched in school about sea creatures. The Parent Thing kind of ate like them, too; it wiggled over the food like a vacuum cleaner.

If she didn't look at it too long she'd be okay. Alice would tell her parents about the things that had been going on at school, how she was talking to a boy online. How she was relieved to be home, actually, because she preferred it this way. Pretended things were normal. It was kind of freeing to be able to speak about it without judgement. While they didn't respond, it did always seem to look at Alice. She had to guess where the face was, things seemed to shift and readjust constantly. Sometimes, big pimple-like bubbles would pop and a thick, bloody puss would get everywhere. It smelled like a dumpster. That was another reason why she stayed at her spot on the stairs. Any closer and she'd vomit.

When the house started getting low on food she would try to find soft chewy things for them to have because she thought they'd like that. Alice often would chew and suck on plastic toys when she was little and figured it couldn't hurt to try. The Parents never spit anything out (not that she thought it could spit, anyway), but they did seem to dislike metal. Screws, bolts, and other bits and bobs piled up in a corner. In a rare moment of laughter, Alice compared it to a litter box.

Maybe due to the lack of protein, her parents started to change. They didn't smell as bad, for one thing. They also lost a lot of their oil sheen and now resembled soft plastic, flesh coloured with bits of pink and red swirling throughout. It seemed sluggish, moving a lot less and noticeably sagging.

The world outside seemed to be quieting down. There were much fewer sirens, helicopters, and yelling than that first day. Alice didn't really care. She was most comfortable at home, even before…ll this. The TV only played static now, but she had plenty of books to read. At least, the power was still working.

While her parents didn't seem to mind the lack of food, Alice was certainly feeling the strain. She had emptied the pantry of anything edible, even tried some of her dad's whiskey before revulsion took over and she spit it out all over the carpet.

Days went by like this: Alice talking to her parents, sleeping a lot, and reading books. She started to have an idea. At first, it was just an intrusive thought she shook away just as fast as it appeared. As the days went on, though, it began to sound more and more appealing. What else was there to do? She had no desire to venture out into the world again. It never welcomed her anyway. She knew her parents loved her and always would. It was an easy decision to make.

On a day not much different than the one before it, Alice woke and put on her favourite hoodie. She brushed her hair (for once) and tidied her room. She spent all morning cleaning the rest of the house, making it presentable. Her mother always said "clean as if the Queen is coming over for tea," and this was the first time she tried to emulate that.

When she was done, she stood at the top of the basement. She looked at the thing that was once her parents, this sad, lopsided mass. The way it seemed to look back at her with recognition. The way she knew, deep inside, her mother and father were there. And waiting for her. She descended the stairs and smiled.

Alice walked over to a semi-clean patch of carpet and laid down on her back. Unable to decide where to put her hands, she eventually settled with them clasped together over her chest. Taking a deep, shaky breath, she waited.

She smelled them before anything else, a slightly sour odour that wasn't as bad as she thought it would be. The mass cautiously touched her feet, as if curious. Then it began sliding up and over her body, just as she had watched it do time and time again to eat.

The feeling was almost indescribable; an all-encompassing heat, as if her entire body was being sunburned. The weight of the creature was welcoming, and Alice felt a vibrant, electric energy course through her. Nothing mattered but this sensation and she wanted it to last forever.

Then it reached her face and things got muddled--she saw a bright flash of red before everything softened, colours mixing and warping from every angle. I can feel the colours everywhere, Alice thought. She felt tears of joy fall from somewhere that didn't exist anymore, until a voice called out to her directly:

Welcome home, Alice.

SEGMENT 6
THE LANDLORD

I'd like to think I'm a practical man. Weighing the pros and cons of situations feels as natural as breathing. I can't say I wasn't freaked the fuck out when those monsters started to show up--ugly sons of bitches--but I saw them for what they really were: a colossal pain in the ass.

See, my bread and butter is the rent checks on several properties I own in and around the city. How am I supposed to collect if everyone is turning into jello?

I mean, okay, not everyone was. In fact--if you squinted really hard it was like nothing was happening at all. People still went to drive-thrus and malls--hell, I got a bill in the mail yesterday. That's got to count for something, right?

On the other hand, some unsettling shit has become the norm on my drive home. Dead cats and dogs littered the street, and you had to play Weasel Stomp to get through. Every block has a burn pile. The news keeps changing their minds about what's contaminated or not. Worst of all is the smell, like dead fish and mould and who knows what else.

Today I'm checking in on a few things. It's a nice day, sun's out, a good day for a drive. Besides the aforementioned annoyances of course.

The first stop is Ted Wheeler. A creepy little man...but he always pays on time, so I can't complain too much. Single--as far as I know--and does some kinda office work. I parked behind his Kia and head on into the backyard. Every one of my properties has a pool, and I charge the tenants extra to maintain them. I do the work myself; no sense putting that money into some shitheads pockets instead of mine (and letting ol' Ted realize he could get it cheaper from them).

"Well hey there Ted, how's it goin'?"

No response, as always, but I like to be cordial.

"God, you look worse every day."

Ted is more pancake than person. Like he had been run over by a steamroller a few times and then casually tossed in the drained pool. He was flat, bloated, and covered in boils. Every few minutes one of them would audibly pop, releasing a thick, pink slime, like rendered chicken. It stunk to high heaven. Now I was, at first, extremely pissed off at Ted. Losing out on rent payments is always irritating. It's not like I can find a new tenant right now anyway.

I cautiously walk around the edge of the pool. Ted doesn't move so much as wiggle like a deflated jellyfish. Picking up the leaf skimmer, I poked the floating mass with the net end of the pole. It sunk into his flesh like butter. When I pulled back, it stretched like a freshly roasted marshmallow, firmly holding the pole in its grip. Sometimes I just like to check on the quality of my product. Not that I really know what's good or bad mind you--but it can't hurt to give him a poke every once and a while. Thankfully there is no chance of Ted "escaping." The pool had been emptied and only contained a couple of inches of rainwater. Old and musty. I've never smelled anything more foul. I would make a joke about my old lady's cunt but there's no one to tell it to.

Sometimes Ted would stretch out and flip over, exposing what I assume to be his backside (he didn't have a dick and balls anymore so I took an educated guess), which was entirely covered in eyeballs. All different colours, all looking directly at me. I fucking hate it. I toss in some ground beef I brought with me and get the fuck out of there.

I know I should be grateful someone out there wants to buy whatever's left of these fuckers. They even have a special hotline, now, where you can report them. Must be a fun job. Oh my god, my boyfriend's melting! Help! What the fuck are they going to do? The cops stopped going to cases when they realized it was fruitless.

Next up is Janice. The most crotchety old woman I've ever had the misfortune of meeting. Even before the world went to shit, she was losing her marbles. One time she told me I had bugs crawling on my face, and I nearly took her out. I know my zit scars aren't pretty, but she didn't have to be a bitch.

Had one of them home nurses come and check on her regularly but not anymore. I'm guessing they've got better things to do now. Hospitals are the only well guarded and safe places these days, can't get anywhere near them. If she went back to work, well, that's her new forever home. That or she bit the dust.

Not sure if it's her age or something but these things don't seem interested in her. She's just been laying there moaning, while it tries to climb out of the pool. Smells like she shit herself. I throw the meat and land a bullseye on the back of her head. My aim gets better every time! Didn't feel like sticking around and watching that blob eat. Hate those slurping noises.

On my way home I pick up some burritos for Jen-- her favourite. You can't say I'm not an attentive husband! I guess some for Bigsby too. The cashier looked pretty out of it; I'm not even sure how they stay in business. Gotta make sure to enjoy the fuck out of this food while it's still around.

"Jen, I'm home!" I call out before realizing my own foolishness. She can't hear me from all the way in the backyard. Gave her an encore as I push through the gate to the back porch.

One of the many advantages of the Event is that my marriage has improved tenfold. You could really say our relationship has...evolved. I wouldn't call what we had love, more like tolerating each other. Jen yells at me a lot less these days. I sit on the edge of the pool while I eat and tell her about my day. Toss down whatever food I brought with me.

Bigsby "sniffed" at it and then began swallowing it whole. Some things never change. Jen kinda mumbled a bit--that's the most I've heard from her in days.

Bigsby's getting stronger every day, looks like he's twice as big now! His fur got all nasty after a few days and started falling off in clumps. Never realized how close their skin colour is to people. Then his bones started poking out of his skin like weird branches, spitting out like they were poison. It was fascinating to watch, the way you could still tell it started as a dog. It's like the wires got crossed down the line and it kept redoing things. Legs? Nah... What about five heads? That sounds about right. Something weird with his teeth now too--he's got about three times as many. Not bad for a dog that started life as a Pomeranian.

Once he's done with Jen I'll call the hotline again.

THE VIRGIN

OUTER-
INCOUNTERS.COM/FORUM/TRUESTORIES/MYFRIE
NDJARED.HTM

I swear this is true. I'm not a creative person and I doubt I
could make it up if I tried.
(Sorry for spelling mistakes, I'm on mobile.)

 I've been having trouble sleeping since this happened
to me. Some people say it helps to talk about things...I
haven't told anyone about it, not even my parents. So instead,
I did some searching and found this forum. It was both
reassuring and terrifying to find people who have gone
through similar experiences.

 Anyway I guess I'll just get to it.

 Last month my friend Jared texted me and told me
he'd met this really hot chick and wanted me to meet her too.
He kept going on and on about how sexy she was and said
she'd definitely fuck me. I should say Jared knew I'm a virgin
and that I'm kind of embarrassed about it, so several times
he's tried to hook me up with girls he knew like, friend-of-a-
friend-of-my-cousin and stuff. It never worked out of course.
it was always awkward and I don't even think half of them
remember who I am. I'm not ugly. At least I don't think so.
I'm just...average.

 I don't want to make it sound like I'm some kind of
freak who's always looking to get laid!! I'm just...open to
the idea of it if the girl is nice and she wants to.

 So Jared really insisted I meet this girl and I have a
hard time saying no to him. Plus I had nothing else going on

that night. So I stupidly sneak out after curfew to meet him at the park. Our town was still fairly safe, we had no major outbreaks and all the roads in and out were guarded 24/7 by the army or whatever. It wasn't something I thought about unless I saw it on the news and even then I tried to ignore it. I hated seeing those things and thinking about how they used to be human.

So I get to Willow's Creek Park and Jared is there, pacing. He seemed really stressed out and like...excited? He was sort of mumbling to himself but I couldn't hear what he was saying. I called out to him and he stopped and quickly walked up to me. He said he'd been waiting for a while, which confused me because he had only texted me like, 10 minutes ago. After some random small talk I noticed Jared kept looking over his shoulder, towards the woods. "Is the chick in the woods? What's she doing?" I asked him. He said she was kind of a hippie and had a little camp set up. "So... she's homeless?" This was sounding less and less appealing by the minute. He got really angry at that and I put my hands up, telling him to slow down, and I apologized. He said something about "getting back to nature" and "connecting with the Earth" or some bullshit. I really wanted to bounce and go to bed but he was super insistent...and he said she'd give us weed.

God I am so dumb. What do they say, "thinking with your dick instead of your brain?" That was me that night.

He led me through this totally random path, with lots of turns. He'd stop at a tree that had seemingly nothing special about it, mumble for a minute, and then take off in a different direction. I used my phone's flashlight cuz it was super fucking dark. I had no signal out here by the way, because I know someone will ask. I had to almost sprint to keep up with Jared, he seemed frantic. I asked him if he was on something and he didn't respond. So... Probably.

After what felt like forever we got to this tiny clearing surrounded by bushes. Jared makes a weird noise to like, announce us or something? A woman's voice responded with another weird noise. I can't describe it very well but it felt off. Like she forgot how to speak and was learning again. You know how people sound after they get hit by a car or something, and it messes with their brain? It was like that. Or when you try to speak while burping. Slow and kind of forced.

We push past the bushes and this is where it gets really fucked up. There's this lady sitting on the ground, with her legs folded beneath herself. She's beautiful, with long brown hair and a huge smile. I couldn't tell how old she was, she looked either in her late teens or early 40's. At the time I blamed it on the smoke from the fire making things look fuzzy. I could see her mouth moving but I couldn't hear any noise come out. The weirdest part was her like, beckoning to us? Like that "come here" motion with her hand.

Jared didn't say anything but he walked forward until he was within reach of the lady. He fell to his knees really hard and started groaning. I couldn't see her from where I was standing but I could see she was leaning back and forth like, swaying almost. Then, I swear to god, Jared pulled his dick out and started jacking off right in front of me. I started yelling at him to stop but it was like he couldn't hear me. My head felt really weird and I wondered if there was something in the smoke, something making us go crazy. I backed up until I was leaning against a tree but I was too scared to turn around. Something felt so incredibly wrong here.

As I watched, Jared was still touching himself but the lady leaned forward and started sucking him off. I was grossed out but at the same time thought it would be good spank bank material for later... don't judge me, OK?? I'm a teenage boy...Sorry I'm getting off track this is the worst part, please believe me that it really happened.

I heard the noise of her mouth on him but it kept getting louder like she was covered in spit or something. This horrible wet slurping. I looked away for a minute and when I turned back I could see her entire face opening up and getting bigger. The skin stretched out over his dick and up to his chest and down to his legs. It rolled out and over stuff in waves and her face kind of fell apart. You could see where the eyes, nose and lips were but they were so far apart now, moving with the rest of the body to cover Jared. He was still moaning and his eyes were closed. I screamed at him but it was like I wasn't even there. It kept moving until it covered his whole front and started going over the top of his head, closing around his back until he was inside her completely. The mouth closed but the lips were now gone, it was a smooth surface. I heard a horrible crunch and the mass started to get smaller and twisted around. I think she was breaking his fucking bones.

It got smaller and smaller... I'm pretty sure she was digesting him. I didn't hear him make any noise after she started eating him so I hope he died fast. I don't want to think about him being awake during all of that. I was terrified and my legs were shaking but I couldn't get them to move. I started punching my thighs like that would help. I heard that voice again, the impossible to make out, forced burp. It took everything I had to look up. The woman was normal again, smiling at me. Doing the same "come here" motion. Something broke in me then and I turned and ran as fast as I fucking could out of the woods. I could still hear her crying out to me but thankfully I don't think she could walk.

It's been a month now and people are starting to forget about Jared. At first, they put up missing person posters and his mom went on the news crying and begging for information about him. Then it sort of tapered off. They asked me about him, since we were friends, and I told them I hadn't seen him for a while. I was too chickenshit to repeat what I saw that night. I don't know why. It feels like it would ruin our town. I don't want to be in one of those places that's always in quarantine and burning shit. I just want things to be normal.

I've started telling people the woods are haunted, that a witch lives there that eats little kids. Hopefully it spreads around and nobody ends up like Jared.

THE ZIT

"God, what is wrong with his face!? What a freak." Two girls snickered, pretending to hide their faces behind a book. When Cassie turned to look at them, hurt and embarrassment were met with an award-worthy eye roll and more laughter. This wasn't the first time Haley and Kayla poked holes in Cassie's saran wrap thin defences, but today's taunting felt extra cold. There's nothing quite as sharp as a teenage girl's insults. The pair had perfected it over years with various subjects; Cassie, in particular, was their favourite to torment.

  Cassie's gaze lowered to the floor as she scurried away, the tears already falling. Despite her efforts her chin stood out like a bullseye. She'd woken up that morning with one of those deep, under the skin pimples just to the side of her lip that hurt like hell but wouldn'twon't come out no matter how much you squeezed. A habitual picker, she took to a sewing needle as her second line of attack. The stabbing was rewarded with the tiniest amount of pus and a trickle of blood. Attempts to push out anything else were fruitless. She moved back from her mirror and surveyed the damage: big as a quarter and tomato red, the pimple seemed to pulse with her heartbeat as she scowled at it. Cassie pushed it down to try to flatten it out...which hurt quite a lot. Her face thoroughly ruined, she caked on concealer, did up the rest of her makeup, and wore a scarf to hide under for good measure.

  H & K weren't the only ones who bullied Cassie, but they were the most consistent. After she had sort-of-but-not-really come out as transgender (she never announced it to the world, but she began dressing like a girl, wearing makeup, and going by Cassie, so people quickly put it together), the insults leveled up to include this. He-she, It, Fag, and otherthe classic go-tos. Many took to moving away when she walked by, like being trans was a communicable disease.

At first it was just irritating, but after a while it chipped away at Cassie. Her thick shell from the years of "normal" bullying cracked and flaked off. She attempted to repair it--hence, the saran wrap--but it was a poor man's substitute. She had simply taken too much and the fight within her dried up. It was easier to avoid as much as possible or retreat to the closest bathroom for an angry cry before composing herself, fixing her makeup for the millionth time and moving on. Cassie had it down to a science. The trick was to push your palms into your eye sockets when you cry, to feel the sting and the ringing in your ears as you press so hard it hurts... aaaaand release. Simple. Effective. Cassie could be a saleswoman. "Our patented new emotional breakdown technique is our best ever. Call now for our instructional DVD and get a free self-harm tool of your choice." Here, she would wave her arm slowly over a table in a flourish, displaying a variety of sharps, alcohol, pills, and her favourite, a toothbrush. "Our operators are waiting for you!" then she'd wink and blow a kiss to the camera. Five stars.

The bell had rung at this point for 2nd period, so Cassie's bathroom retreat was thankfully empty. The art building was the preferred choice, being a single stall with a not completely cracked mirror, but the main building's first floor by English class would do. She took the stall closest to the wall and began getting better acquainted with the newest graffiti while she calmed down.

She was tired of this routine. Adults love to say high school is the best time of your life and you should enjoy it while you can. Cassie knew they were all liars and just missed when they didn't have to pay bills. It's not like she was learning anything useful; all teachers cared about was if you memorized the information. If it went out the other end

34

as soon as the test was over, it didn't matter. Their job here was done. Cassie just barely skirted by, anyway. She was too focused on surviving the rest of her life to care about Social Studies.

Okay, here we go. Patent pending cry initiated. Cassie dug her palms into her face and silently wailed. Her fresh tears mixed with her already ruined eyeliner and stung, making her cry more. She sat like this for a few minutes, resting her elbows on her knees. When it ran its course, she took out a pocket mirror to redo her smokey eyes before stopping dead. The pimple had grown, now resembling an engorged tick embedded in Cassie's face. She cautiously touched it with a finger and it wiggled. Something firm inside strained against her skin.

Fighting the urge to simultaneously hurl and rip off her face off, she threw herself out of the stall to the bigger mirror. "What the fuck!!" Cassie pressed her face up to get a better look. The zit moved again. Hysterical now, she fumbled in her purse for something, anything, before settling on a mechanical pencil. Staring down at this mundane object and potential relief from the horrible growing wriggling inside her face, Cassie became overwhelmed. She sobbed while holding it up to her cheek, losing her composure and backing away for a few seconds. The pain grew worse with every passing moment. "Okay, okay, you can do this. Just get it out."

Her right hand came up again, aiming the pencil like a needle at the growing mass, the other braced so hard on the sink's edge that her knuckles turned white. With the graphite tip touching the lump, Cassie sucked in a breath and broke the skin. It tore away like tissue paper with a stream of white chunky mush splatting the mirror and stippling down her shirt.

She couldn't hold it back now, vomiting hot cereal chunks to add to the cottage cheese falling out of her open wound. Screaming, she dashed back to the toilet–, dripping various fluids on the floor as she went–. Collapsing and collapsed in front of the same seat from several minutes earliera few minutes ago. Instead of ebbing, the pain became sharper, like little spines pushing in and out of her flesh as the goo fell steadily fell into the bowl. Cassie wouldn't dare open her eyes, the smell was bad enough. Like the time her toe got infected, mixed with an outhouse. The pressure around her wound suddenly blossomed and her vision blacked out before she heard a loud plop.

Cassie froze. She was sweating profusely, vomit and who knows what else caking her face. She dared to glance into the toilet. A flash of movement, a splash and that was it--she scrambled to slam the lid down and flush as fast as she could. The water gurgled and went down, refilling without any unusual sounds. Whatever it was must have gone down...right?

"Just my imagination. It must be. It was nothing. I... I need to get the fuck out of here." Cassie fell back, staring at the closed toilet. There was no reasonable explanation for whatever the hell just happened. A fresh sniffle and new string of tears cut through the mess on her face. With any luck she could clean herself up and go home. School didn't matter after what just happened.

The toilet lid rattled. Before she could lunge forward to hold it down, a torrent of water and sludge burst out with the intensity of a fire hydrant, covering Cassie from head to toe in body waste and whatever she flushed a moment ago. The force pushed her backwards and slammed the back of her head on the porcelain sink, causing the tiles and fixtures behind her to smash one-by-one on the floor before everything faded.

When Cassie awoke, she felt different. Her entire body felt warm and tingly and not entirely unpleasant. She rose from the floor in a smooth motion, spinning towards the only remaining mirror. Looking back at her was a tall slender woman with the longest hair she'd ever seen. Huge strands gently blew as if in a constant breeze. From the waist down the figure spread out like a huge, ruffled skirt that touched the floor, all the same nude shade matching the skin. Cassie squinted to try to get a better look, but her eyes wouldn't cooperate. "Is that...me?" As if responding the hair flicked upwards, and Cassie held out a hand to touch it. Instead of fibres the strand was a giant tube, pink and veiny. Slick with mucus the "hair" flowed through her fingers and rejoined its sisters. Running her hands up and down her chest, she shivered. The warmth she felt was intoxicating, like being wrapped in a blanket after a long day. She was suddenly overwhelmed with the desire to share this feeling with everyone and anyone.

As if on cue, Haley and Kayla pushed into the bathroom. They screamed. Cassie held out her arms and smiled.

38

THE PATROL

Sean, Derrick, and I were out on patrol when it happened. Sean's car still had some gas after the last patrol, and we'd seen more of them in the last few days, so it felt right to go. Wish I hadn't.

It was a cool September night and the roads were, of course, totally empty. Sometimes, I forget about the state of things and just zone out while we drive around. There weren't really any set directions for patrols; just make your way through a couple of blocks around the perimeter and check for meatsacks.

Drive-bys were the easiest and safest way to patrol. You got your windows rolled up, and you can peel out of there pretty damn fast when you need to. Guns were a bit harder to come by these days, but you got special access for patrols. Safety of the community and whatnot. Sean had his on the passenger seat, while Derrick and I sat in the back with ours. I wasn't the best shot, but you didn't have to be with the Outers.

Outers was what we called them now; but back in the day, when it first started, they were the Inside-Outers. You ever seen one of those cartoons where someone gets turned inside out? Looks kinda like that. All wet flesh and organ meat moving around. The name stuck, but as things do, it got shorter. Faster to say when shit goes down, I suppose.

I didn't know they had such reach. That they could move their bodies like that. Hope someone made a note of it for records. I certainly can't. I hope the boys remember me, at least for a little while. I don't want them to think of me like that. Like one of those things.

All in all, the night was going pretty good; brought a six-pack for the occasion, Sean found an old zipcase of CDs we popped in the player and we were enjoying ourselves. For the first time in a long time.

Sean was ripping around corners and when we came across the old Crescent Hill Mall, we saw a chance to have a little fun. He started doing donuts in the parking lot while me and Derrick both whooped and cheered. The sound of the wheels and the smell of the rubber on the pavement were some of the last things I remember and try to hold on to. It gets harder to think every day now.

The mall had a liquor store, and I was buzzed enough I wanted to see if they still had any. You could get lucky and find canned food and bottled stuff, depending on where you were and how bad things had gotten when it all went down. Last month, I got a box of pasta and I swear it was the best goddamn macaroni I ever tasted in my life.

I got out of the car and shoved my pistol down the back of my pants. Sean turned the volume up louder and started air drumming on the steering wheel. I think for a moment we kinda forgot about how things were now and were thinkin' about how things were then.

I wasn't paying attention, stumbled on a goddamn rock, and had to catch myself on a car hood. That fucking rock. If everything that made me me is gone now. If I have any feeling left in my soul, it is a burning hatred for that rock. How the fuck did it get in the parking lot? How long had it been there, perfectly waiting for my foot? Piece of shit.

I heard a familiar wet noise, and my breath hitched. Then I smelled it. That sickly sweet, rotten smell they all had. Even though we all knew by now that they didn't have eyes, didn't track like that, I still moved my head as slowly as I could. I didn't want to look at it but I knew I had to. Looked to the back of the car and there it was...an Outer.

40

The worst thing about Outers is how much you can tell, deep down, they were once a human. Got all the right parts, I guess. Well...most of them. They are vaguely person-shaped, but like you smooshed one down a bit between your fingers. Don't know how they held together, to be honest. The intestines were the worst part. Did we really have that much in us? I don't know how it fits. All ropey and pulsing with whatever it ate last. The smell of rotten meat and shit wafted over me and I gagged.

I clapped my hands over my mouth and tried to be as quiet as possible. People say they hunt by multiple senses, so I was worried it would smell the booze on me. It kept, like...moving its head up, like it was trying to sniff me out. I backed up and caught my foot on that rock again, letting out a yelp without meaning to. That's when it struck.

The tentacle-like arm whipped out and grabbed me right above my wrist. It burned like acid and felt sticky. I screamed, but pulled away easily enough. Turned around and ran back towards Sean's car as fast as my legs would carry me.

They both saw me coming and froze. I was yelling, waving my arms. I just wanted to get the fuck out of there. Derrick looked at me, then looked at my arm. Saw the red welt and whatever that drool-spit shit they leave on you is called. Derrick pulled his gun. Then Sean followed suit. I stopped running and still had my arms in the air like I was being put under arrest. Sean made a weird face, like a grimace and an apology all wrapped into one shitty present. I fell to the ground as they shot me, once, twice, I don't know how many times. I lost count. Didn't hurt as much as I expected. Fucking waste of bullets, though. Could have just shot me once and got it over with. By that point, it was already too late.

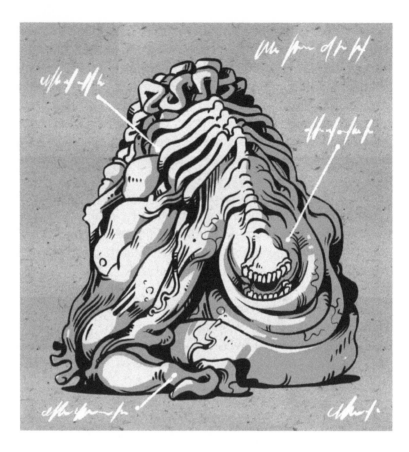

My ears rang, but through it I could still hear them arguing with each other for what seemed like hours. hen there was the distinct rumble of their car leaving me, forever.

"Please…" I tried to say, but it came out as a weird gurgle and I coughed up a lot of blood. I was shaking like a leaf. I tried to look at my hand, but it was all fuzzy. Everything was fuzzy. Then it got worse. I felt this hot wetness drip down my face and everything went black. I tried to scream again and put my hand on my face. Where the fuck were my eyes?! I felt around the socket, and it was just...mush.

Then my insides were burning. I'd never been in so much pain. Every nerve in my body was on fucking fire and I cried and cried; but at this point, I don't think I had tears anymore. I felt like I was being dipped into a pit of acid. I don't know how I knew–maybe the last remnant of my brain–but my bones were dissolving. Heard...no felt a huge crack of what must have been my arm bone snapping as I pushed myself up on my knees and tried to get up. All my senses were fading.

I didn't want to feel this. I didn't want to know that this is fucking happening to me. Tried to lift my arm and it sloughed off with sickening ease. Everything hurts. Please, God, if you're up there. Just let it end.

It's getting harder everyday now. I can feel my senses fading. The worst part is I can now feel others. I'm not alone in here.

THE TATTOOIST

Tom stood in the kitchen, meticulously cleaning the slab of dead flesh. He wiped off the excess oil and trimmed the fat, prepping the skin for work. Once he'd done this process a few times it became almost automatic, with his mind drifting off to avoid the stench.

"You know," said Emma as she watched, far enough away not to smell the meat, yet close enough to gawk all the same. "When I agreed to this I wasn't expecting rotting pigskin in my fridge."

He sighed inaudibly and prepped the stencil. "You know if I'm hoping to make a career of this, I have to take it seriously. How is it any different from your makeup? They test that shit on animals."

"Well, my palettes don't smell like ass." She idly scratched the skin under her nose before leaving. Tom wondered if Emma's nostrils were permanently flared.

Having removed the stencil now that its job was finished, he sat down, firing up the gun and began tattooing the pigskin.

The best substitute for human skin is, without a doubt, pig. It's not a perfect match, but it's better than the fake stuff Tom bought once online. Artificial skin is more like a combination of gauze and mouse pad material. It's too spongy and doesn't give you the same resistance. Real skin needs the right amount of pressure to get in the dermis layer, but not so hard you'll have a customer screaming. If your pigskin is squealing you've got even more problems.

Since the skin is usually just cut off and discarded, Tom has found a few pounds for cheap. He'd fill up the freezer and defrost the chunks one at a time while he worked. Apprenticeships were hard to come by these days and he had to improve somehow--Emma was staunchly anti-ink so that was out of the question. Tom was already a colouring book of random designs, memories of his best (and worst) decisions. A macaroni noodle while drunk, various band logos...plus a burn shaped so much like a heart he couldn't help but go over it with ink.

Dead flesh also doesn't move like the living. It's tough, having lost the elastic nature given to it by blood flowing through the veins. It also dries out quickly. Tom would tattoo for a half-hour, then pop it in the fridge and take a break.

Today he was working on a simple cursive exercise, trying to nail down a consistent depth and speed. The word Everlasting. He washed his hands several times before checking on Emma.

She was, as he figured, in front of her mirror. Makeup had always been Emma's passion, and she was quite good at it. Even achieved a decent following on social media. One of her trademarks was her anti-ageing tips. She glanced at Tom and continued applying foundation.

"Done with Miss Piggy?"

"Yeah, for now." He leaned over and gave her a small kiss on the shoulder before resting his chin. "Is that new?"

"Mhm, I got an email from this company asking if I wanted to try their new line. Give my honest opinion, you know."

Tom tried his best to keep up with the types of products Emma used. He knew a few things, like how primer comes before concealer, but much of it remained mumbo jumbo. "What's the brand?" He asked.

"Natural Skin Solutions. Generic ass name but seems all right so far. It's apparently made from sustainable minerals and emollients in South America."

46

"Hmm." He'd lost interest. "There's pig in the fridge. Don't eat it."

Emma scoffed. "Like I would." She rubbed her cheeks with a sponge and began blending. "This stuff is so smooth. Smells weird too."

Tom hmm'd again and went to watch TV. They'd started up a new season of Stuck Together, where hot 20-somethings full of piss, drama and vinegar shared a house together. He thought it seemed in bad taste considering current events but figured maybe it was filmed earlier. There was an unspoken consensus to continue on with life as though nothing was the matter, but it was working as well as ignoring a dog mauling your leg. Eventually, Tom drifted off to sleep.

When Tom awoke it was past midnight. He stumbled off to bed after a quick pee. He always felt bad about nodding off, but Emma usually woke him before she went to bed herself.

Instead, he found her right where she'd been hours before: applying makeup.

"Are you still not done? It's late."

Emma was rubbing her cheeks and twisting her body this way and that, extremely focused on the mirror. "I think I was allergic to something in that makeup. My skin feels all weird. I've been trying to fix it." She pulled under her eyelid and the flesh sagged without bouncing back. Then she tried the other, before bursting into tears. "I look like a freak!" Emma's voice was becoming thicker, full of spit. She turned to look at Tom and he stifled a laugh. Everything from the nose down was like a deflated balloon. With her cheeks hanging past her mouth, she looked like a dog. Tears streaming down her face, she asked him how bad it was.

"Uhm." He pretended to cough. "I'll be real with ya, it doesn't look so good. Do you want to go to the hospital?"

Even with several layers of wet cream on her face, Tom could see Emma grow pale. "I can't let anyone see me like this!" Before he could say anything else she ran into the bathroom, locking the door behind her.

"Well…if you need anything …" He trailed off, unsure what else to do and settled in for the night. Sleep didn't come as easily this time, as every few minutes, he laughed at the absurdity of the situation. Tom worked through how to convince Emma to see a doctor in the morning before passing out.

Not only did Emma refuse to see a medical professional, but she also refused to even leave the bathroom. Clothes, snacks and lots of her makeup went with her, gathered when Tom was asleep or out of the apartment. He called all her friends, and they couldn't get anything out of Emma either; she just left their messages as read but wouldn't reply. Tom was beginning to lose patience. He missed the privacy and comfort of his own toilet. After a week of this, he told Emma through the door that he was calling the cops in the morning to break it down the door whether she liked it or not. He was met with stony silence. An obvious odour of bleach and excrement wafted from under the door, making Tom retch in his mouth.

Stuck Together once again rounded out Tom's night. He was only half paying attention when he realized everyone on the show was either crying or yelling. He turned up the volume and tried to catch the details.

"…You realize how fucking stupid that sounds, right? You really expect us to believe that?" Shaun, the loveable jock of this season was shouting and pacing in front of a vidscreen, where a stuffy-looking producer spoke to them.

"We try not to let contestants know about the outside world during the show but we felt this was unique circumstances..." Tom had never seen a man look so uncomfortable. Even though he and The Fun House members were likely thousands of miles apart, he wouldn't look at any of them. Instead, he wiped his face, eyes to the ceiling or off-screen, likely reading from a script or coached by higher-ups.

"My family's fucking dead?!" Gracie, a beach blonde in an oversized hoodie, looked ready to spit fire. "How can you sit there and say that with a straight face? That they melted? This has to be a joke. It's scripted, they're testing us!" Several others were nodding. "Whoever falls for this is getting sent home, right?"

"This is not a joke. The entire west coast has been declared uninhabitable, from Washington to Nevada. Arizona has begun evacuations. Remaining in the Fun House is the safest option for everyone."

Tom simultaneously felt jealous and sad for the group. The literal plague was taking place while they sipped cocktails and fooled around. It wasn't all that different from the people who sought to avoid the news, pretending it doesn't affect them. But then again, wasn't he doing the same thing? Who's going to want tattoos at a time like this? Maybe no one. But it kept Tom going. He couldn't just sit around and wait for the world to end. The next day always came, and with it, the need to eat, to socialize, to keep his mind and body focused. The fact that all of humanity was going through this crisis together was somehow comforting, even if the specifics were wildly different. Life goes on whether you like it or not.

When he looked back, Shaun, Gracie and the other housemates were trashing the Fun House. Throwing chairs, ripping couch cushions apart and smashing every hidden camera they could find. A ticker appeared on the bottom of the screen: WE ARE PRESENTING THIS FOOTAGE

WITHOUT ALTERATIONS. CONTACT WITH CONTESTANTS WAS LOST AND ANY ATTEMPTS TO REACH THEM HAVE BEEN UNSUCCESSFUL. THE ENTIRE STUCK TOGETHER TEAM WISHES THEM THE BEST DURING THESE UNPRECEDENTED TIMES. Eventually, the screen turned to static as the last camera was ripped from the wall.

Wired, Tom headed to the last open bar in the neighbourhood to calm down. Nobody could talk about anything other than the Merge Infection. At this point, everyone knew at least one person affected. Family, friends. The red string of fate cuts through rich and poor. In the end, we're all in the meat grinder. After the last call, Tom picked up a 6-pack of Mickeys and drove home, the rising sun bearing down on his back.

Force of habit had him sneak into the apartment, closing the door as quietly as possible. Silent entrance dashed as his senses were assaulted by a blast of rot and the instinct to cover his nose and mouth was too quick. The bottles smashed on his boots, splashing alcohol and shards of glass everywhere. He shuffled backwards and cursed. Thankfully one bottle survived the disaster, and he planned on drinking it immediately.

Tiptoeing into the kitchen to get some paper towel, Tom froze. The fridge was wipe open. Hunched over, a person stood in the light, a silhouette of darkness. No other lights were on. A slurping, wet sound cut through the silence.

Unnerved, but nonetheless happy to see her out of the bathroom's confines, Tom stepped closer. "Emma? Are you OK? If you're hungry, babe, I can make you something to eat, you don't have to go through the fridge…"

She turned to face Tom. It took his eyes a moment to adjust. Emma held a slab of pig skin in both hands, tearing off chunks to eat. Slimy vegetables, crunched up condiment bottles and pickle juice covered the floor, streaks of grime painted her legs. With a horrifying RRRrrippp another hunk of pork was torn off, Emma chewing around it like a cow with cud.

"It's not working. I needed more skin, Tom." Her voice was barely recognisable, and he had to strain to even understand her. Spittle and clumps of fat blew out of her mouth with every word.

"You can't...you can't eat that. It's not safe to eat, it's not even cooked..." He reached out with his free hand to grab her, to do something, anything, to make her stop. "We really need to take you to the hospital."

Within reach of her now, Tom bit his tongue to keep from yelling. Emma's face had peeled back, the muscle tissue underneath peeking through. It hung down in a loose flap in line with her eyebrows. Her neck was pushed forward, and she tilted her head upwards to see, like the brim of a hat. She made a gargled, strained noise, drool frothing at the corners of her lips. The movement caused the flap to sway, before it sloughed down and off her face, rolling into lasagne waves before landing in a pile of ketchup and squished berries.

Emma's face was too far gone to save. She spent weeks at the hospital before a Dr. approached us with a silicone mask, some new kind of artificial skin, she'd said. It wasn't perfect, but it was better than seeing those endless gums and horrible chattering teeth. We're still getting used to it, but Emma seems happy–the mask is safe to use makeup on, and she's gained a new stream of followers.

DAILY BRIEFING, APRIL 25th

Laurie stands up to the podium, her notes laid before her. The ASL interpreter stands off to her left. A voice in her earpiece relays that the live stream will begin in 3 minutes. Although these daily progress reports–updating the nations on the Merge Infection–had become just another routine, Dr. Laurie Forrester still hated them. Her time was precious, with new projects and regulations coming in almost as fast as new infections. It felt like a new Scientific Age had begun and that anything was possible. The loss of life was, of course, tragic, but what plan doesn't have snags along the way? Her career had certainly been full of highs and lows.

"You're good to go in 5, 4, 3…" Brought back to the present, Laurie cleared her throat and double-checked her notes.

"Good morning, bonjour, and buenos dias everyone. Before I begin, I'd like to remind you that we have both French and Spanish re-streams of these briefings for your convenience. Full transcripts will be available later in the day.

"Let me start this morning by giving an update on the current totals…" She checks the first paper and reads. "941 new cases, and 300 confirmed deaths in the past 24 hours. Several new clusters have been spotted in the San Diego area, so residents, please take all necessary precautions. Our teams are already working to contain the affected zones.

"As we gradually and carefully work our way through this pandemic, some of you may have questions or concerns about compensation if you or your family members have been Infected. Rest assured, we are working on a new system to deal with this, and will have details in the coming weeks. Remember to isolate for the recommended time if you have been in close contact. And keep in mind that not all Infections are fatal. We would like to share some good news by providing an update on the case of Miguel Esparza, an 8-year-old boy who lost an arm to the Infection, but is now recovering with his family by his side, thanks to the help of our Derma research."

Laurie knew the screen would cut to footage they shot of little Miguel testing his new artificial arm, his parents smiling with tears in their eyes. She winced internally, thinking how the arm had gone berserk hours later, the boy unwillingly smashing his mother's face in. She flipped through her notes for a moment, centering herself before speaking again.

"As you know, we are making decisions on a day-by-day basis. Our priority, firstly, is to curb the rate of infections before we create a vaccine. We are consistently adjusting to allow citizens keep a semblance of normality while also keeping people safe. With your help, we can get through this. Thank you, merci, and gracias."

"Cut! OK, thanks, Dr. Laurie. We'll see you tomorrow." They were already waving her offstage to set up the afternoon press conferences.

Finally, she thought. Today would be preliminary testing for a new Derma system, and Laurie had the perfect candidate already picked out.

SEGMENT 12
THE PILE

Dr. Christensen has asked me to keep this journal--more a diary really, to record my thoughts during our experiments. He says since most computers are out of commission, written records will become the standard again. I agreed, but with a bit of trepidation. I haven't written in a diary since I was a little girl. It's a bit strange to be writing again…but I suppose these are strange times.

    The date is October 14th, [REDACTED]. Today we continued Pressure Sensitivity tests on the specimens. It's becoming increasingly difficult to find fresh subjects for our studies. The Dr. has "suggested" I head out tomorrow with a bodyguard and do some fieldwork. He wants me to observe the large formation in the nearby town of [REDACTED]. I cannot say I am looking forward to venturing outside of the compound but there is no one else. Dr. Christensen and I are technically the only researchers in the facility with experience from before the Event.

    Specimen no.11 has proven to be more resilient than previous subjects, withstanding 750 pounds of pressure to the main body for approximately 5 minutes. As we do not want to lose the subject, testing was halted; though it appeared that it could withstand more. As the weight was lowered, noted in previous tests, a yellow, milky excretion discharged from various pores along the body. The general shape returned after several minutes once the weight was removed. It behaves quite like a sponge in this way. No vocalizations are observed, just the natural body sounds (gurgling, etc.) As the whole body is a myriad of different skin tones and contusions it is difficult to gauge whether it sustained any damage during the process. As always, there is the unmistakable odor of rotting meat. I will never get used to the smell of them, even behind glass and barriers. The janitorial crew has their work cut out for them.

Unfortunately, one of the earlier specimens, no.7, had to be disposed of today. The level of decomposition was too great to continue testing. Tissue samples were taken before the specimen was broken up and used as nourishment for no.10 and no.11. No change in behavior was noted after consumption, although no.11 did seem to "pause" before it began eating. Was this a remnant of its former humanity? It's impossible to say. The tests on the brain stems remain inconclusive when we can find them. Several (no.3, no.7, and no.10) have not had anything resembling a brain at all. The organs contained within seem to be at random. Some have a full set. Some have multiples or will be missing presumably "important" bowels.

It is strange and definitely against my teachings to have a "favourite", but I'm afraid I have no other way to describe it. (Perhaps by writing this down it will become clearer to me.) No.11 is…different, from the others. It bears no significant visual differences from other formations, and this is most unscientific of me to admit, but I sense an awareness in it. There almost appears to be a reluctance when the daily tests conclude, and I could swear I witnessed it reach for the implements on more than one occasion. As if it is growing more resilient to the tests and desires more. I find myself… Proud of it, in a way. I have never felt the pull of motherhood and doubt I will (although we are encouraged to pair up, or at the very least, freeze our eggs and sperm) and this is laughable, but I see it as a child, growing and learning. To see how much it can endure and recover, stronger, is one of my greatest joys. Perhaps I will speak to the Dr. about overseeing its progress personally.

Today is the day I set forth outside. Johann has been assigned to me as my bodyguard. He is a dependable man, so I have no qualms with this. It is a pity my trip is the same day as the scheduled conductivity tests, as I do find the muscles and ligaments of the specimens straining through their flesh fascinating. No.11's test will be sometime while I am away, and this gives me a twinge of envy. Maybe I can convince Dr. Christensen to move the next one to a time where I will be available to assist.

Johann and I donned our protective suits and took one of the jeeps. He has a standard-issue flamethrower and sidearm, while I have been given a stun pistol, in case I find any suitable subjects to bring back with us. The jeep has room for several, but as they all seem to coalesce when placed in a confined space it should be no issue. If we should get so lucky! I also have a pair of binoculars and this journal with me.

Upon approaching the outlining area (I find myself wanting to refer to it as this formation's "territory" although they do not behave in a way that indicates this is the case) the smell becomes noticeable, even through our masks. We have left the jeep in a secluded alleyway, covered with a tarp. There are no survivors in this area so there is no fear it will be stolen; however, it is a precaution, and Johann seems very much a "by the book" type.

After trekking for a few miles, we decided to use the roof of a parking garage as our base of operations for the remainder of the day. It was a fair distance away from the action, as it were, and allowed us to see "who" was coming should one of them get curious and venture up here. Thankfully, they are quite docile in nature until they get within striking range so I am not worried.

After setting up, I begin my observations. Johann tells me many people refer to this formation as "The Pile" --

crude, but the name has begun to stick, so I will be referring to it as such from here on.

I would estimate The Pile to be over 350 feet long, half that in height. It resembles the smaller specimens in many aspects, skin tone, general body composition. I assume, due to mass, it is too heavy to allow travel, as I have not witnessed it move more than general undulations. Curiously, I surveyed a smaller body and who approached it, stopping just as they touched. I assume some sort of communication took place--perhaps chemical? This interaction lasted for several minutes. Then quite suddenly the lesser creature was sucked in and seemed to become part of The Pile. I speculate this is how it feeds, by absorbing others of its kind. There is no visible mouth, nor anything that could be called a face.

What happened next was beyond shocking, but I will do my best to describe it exactly as I witnessed it. Johann touched my shoulder and spoke quietly to me: "There is a vehicle coming from the east. Do not make a sound." He must have exceptionally good hearing, or I was simply too distracted by my writing to notice. Very poor oversight on my part.

He was right, of course, and soon I saw what he was talking about--a large, armored truck came into view and skidded to a stop a short distance away from The Pile. Several figures exited, all men from what I could see. Curiously, one of them appeared to be wearing a robe made of pieces of leather crudely stitched together. Quite shoddy handmanship, it's covered in holes.
Upon closer inspection...No.
It's made of faces. Human faces.

The man held himself like he was of great importance. The second person seemed to be his own armed guard, as he was in full SWAT gear with guns and some sort of extendable pole. He pulled open one of the rear doors and dragged someone out, bound and gagged. The man in the...skins began speaking in a very deliberate manner, although I could not make out any words. He placed his hand on the prisoner's face, cupping his cheek. Then he signaled to the guard, who then pushed the man forward with the pole until he was within striking distance of The Pile.

The two of them stepped back and watched as their charge struggled on the ground, thrashing against the ropes that tied him. He was facing away from the mass. The Pile reached out with several tentacles as if curious. Each resembled a slug, with a viscous liquid surrounding each. One of them dragged down the man's side, pulling clothes and skin off as easily as slicing butter. Although he wore a gag I do not doubt that he was screaming, as his movements became erratic and he tried to push away. More tentacles appeared and wrapped around him until I could not see the body anymore. They constricted and pulled back, leaving a trail of blood and mucus on the pavement. The robed man bowed deeply with his arms out.

Both men turned to leave but then the bodyguard stopped and touched the robed man. He reacted in anger, yelling and pointing. Then from our vantage point we could see The Pile reaching out again, faster and with intent. It picked up the bodyguard and constricted him like a snake. He flailed and screamed while the other man stood still, his hands in prayer. Suddenly the tendrils twisted and the bodyguard exploded, blood and gore raining down from above.

The remaining man fell to his knees. The Pile snatched him as well, this time simply crushing the man. Blood spurted in between the tendrils wrapped around him. Then they retreated back into the main body.

Thankfully I doubt they spotted us as they were focused on this...offering? Johann seems unnerved and wants us to leave. I am remiss to return to the compound without any new specimens, but I am also in no position to argue. The smell has become noticeably stronger. I chanced one last look at The Pile…Something's different. The body is covered in red, raised bumps like hives. A strange pollen has begun to carry on the wind. There is something here. Something new.

THE PRIEST

"The way of all flesh is Unity. Someday, under the light of our everlasting Sol, we will be together in body. Today, you have that honour: to become One with Our Grace, Soma, the Holy Marrow from which we are all birthed and will all return. May you take glory in union. Emerge from the Womb of your body and become unified. For in the flesh we are complete."

Tannum placed his right hand on the cheek of the Beloved, letting his mind go blank and relishing in the feel of his flesh touching another. It was clammy, it was human, and it was wonderful, as it always was. Then he raised his chin towards Andrew in acknowledgement. Stepping back, hands clasped together to observe the Joining. He felt at peace, as he always did, witnessing another soul become one with Soma. His turn would come soon when his work was finished. This life was temporary, after all, and underneath the shackles of individualism there was eternal flesh. Under our layers, we were all the same and would become One again. As it was, as it should be, Tannum thought to himself.

Brought back from his wandering mind he watched the proceedings with a small smile resting on his lips. Soma stretched out her arms to welcome the Beloved, to caress him. Unfortunately, not every soul is ready, for this one began to react violently, kicking and yelling as his layers came undone. Soon, it would not matter. He was wrapped in the arms of love and acceptance, and made whole. Tannum did the ceremonial bow, wide and deep to pay respects. "You are complete." He said this more to himself than anyone.

"We must go, Preserver Tannum." Andrew looked awkward, as he always did after a Joining.

There was a pause. "Yes, of course." No, he wanted to say, I will stay here and finally be free. I cannot stand being apart from Her any longer, from Unity, from love and warmth. I would give anything to no longer deal with this tedium, these people, this horrible existence. "Of course."

As his mind once again wandered from the here and now, Andrew gently touched his shoulder and retreated just as quickly. No one was meant to touch a priest, only to be touched by a priest. "A-Apologies, Preserver! Something...something is happening to The Pile!"

"Don't you dare call Her that crude name, you are in the presence of GOD-" Tannum hissed, recovering from the two blasphemies at once. He had never felt so disrespected. "You will be flayed for this. You will never know the pleasures of the Joining-"

But his words were caught short as Andrew was whipped from his sight in a flash of movement and a scream. Tannum's eyes snapped back to his God. There, above him, his sinful companion was held in more tentacles than the priest had ever seen. He was crying, begging while the flesh of Soma touched him, skin tearing, sagging and burning away. Tightening their grip, and pulling, pulling. Time began to slow to a crawl as Andrew was stretched to his limits, every fibre of his being torn apart. What was once a man was a spattering of organs spilling on the broken pavement, bones clinging desperately to muscles of red. So much red.

Tannum sank to his knees and wept. "Thank you," he said through tears, "for this blessing."

The Pile did not respond, yet it also seemed to understand him. A single strand reached towards the priest, gentle, curious. The smell of it was overwhelming, all-encompassing, stinging his already wet eyes. Unable to help himself, Tannum reached for the one thing he wanted in all of the universe.

His God did not hesitate.

"Oh," he thought, for his voice could no longer speak.

His flesh was on fire, a thousand suns at once. The strand enveloped him, pulling at everything it touched like a cat's tongue. Tannum tried to break free, but his body was weak, so weak. Every part of him screamed. He blinked away what he thought were tears, but it was the remnants of his eyes, mixing with blood and something else. Without sight, the agony became worse.

"Oh," his heart cried, for it could no longer beat.

He was on the flesh and in the flesh, every part of his being torn apart to be reassembled and reconstituted, to be used and reused. There was no voice of God, just the unending rending of bodies screaming with voices long gone. There is no Unity here, Tannum strained and pushed and tried to resist even as what remained of his form was destroyed down to the atomic level.

"Oh." his body shuddered, as it ceased to be.

SEGMENT 14
THE SCIENTIST

The following are written transcripts of VHS cassettes found in the lab at [REDACTED].

TAPE 01_INTRODUCTION

A man in a lab coat with short grey hair and glasses stands in centre frame. Behind him sits a whiteboard covered in various diagrams.

"Hello! My name is Dr. Colin Christensen. I know, I know, alliteration… you can thank my parents for that." Dr. Christensen chuckles and rubs his hands together before lightly clapping.

"Now! If you're watching this video, that means you have been selected as a subject for our upcoming program. I know you didn't exactly 'volunteer' for this…" he says, making air quotations. "But I assure you it is a privilege, and, in fact, an honour to be chosen for this task. Unfortunately, we don't have any way to contact your family to let them know…the postal service isn't up and running anymore! We will keep your name and details on file, of course. We keep diligent records here!"

Dr. Christensen takes a pointer from his pocket and turns to the whiteboard.

"To get to the meat and potatoes of the program...apologies for the pun. Our research here is of the utmost importance to the future of humanity. You, by now, are at least aware of the beings known as Clusters, Outers, Blobs---the name is not important---these are our subjects. With your help, we can take one step closer to solving the puzzle of their existence and the Event that birthed them into this world."

"As an honorary member of our research team, your task is simple: to determine what separates us from them. I promise it's not a big philosophical endeavour! In fact, it's already begun. You've been injected with cells from our star patient and will soon join it as a sort of... roommate! Won't that be fun?"

He smiles and points to a series of drawings on the whiteboard. The first features a simple human silhouette standing in place. In the second, a needle injects a substance into their body. Then a series of question marks lead into a rudimentary blob shape. The words "SUBJECT > INJECTION OF CELLS > UNKNOWN > SUCCESS!!!" are written next to the drawings.

The doctor smiles and waves at the camera.
"See you soon!"

TAPE 02_OBSERVATIONS

A static camera faces an enclosure containing a "Peeled" specimen. The cement walls are bare and a small pile of what appears to be clothing sits in one corner. There are many layers of glass and plastic separating the cell from the room the camera is in. Dr. Christensen can be heard somewhere off-camera.

"Just checking in on our favourite patient today! They had a very big day yesterday with their new friend. Take note, Henry: from first glance, it appears to have consumed the new subject completely. You'll notice no.11 doesn't like to eat clothes--I still haven't figured out how it separates the organic and inorganic so easily. There is some damage to the garments, of course, but they're shockingly intact for being next to melting flesh! We'll have someone collect them later for testing. Remember Henry! After a patient has eaten--for lack of a better word--they become extra aggressive, so it necessitates a waiting period before we disturb them in any way."

"Yes, doctor. I'll supervise the cleanup team myself." The voice sounds like a younger man, presumably Henry.

"Now then! There's something I need to discuss with you…"
The voices become quieter here and move away from the camera microphone slightly.

"As you might already know, Mary has not returned from her fieldwork so we'll need to send a corps unit and discuss the matter with her replace--wait, is that camera still running!? Turn that damned thing off!"

There is some muffled speaking as a blurry figure moves towards the camera and stops the recording.

TAPE 03_ARMS

"Look, look at this. It's evolved!" Dr. Christensen speaks quickly.

The camera is shaking and going intermittently out of focus. It points at another containment cell, this one housing a Peeled that exhibits a huge number of arms that flail and twitch violently, making determining the number of limbs impossible. One slams against the glass, making the digits visible momentarily: long and slender, the skin heavily mottled. The picture judders, taking several moments to readjust.

"I promise you, it was not like this yesterday. The structure is completely different, and it appears to be growing even more limbs as time passes. It is truly a

Hecatonchire...the hundred-armed giants of Greek myths. The process of mutation was completely internal; none of our cameras picked up anything out of the ordinary until the arms quite literally burst from within the subject! It's wonderful!"

The camera focuses on the main body as the skin bubbles and erupts, discharging blood and pus. Fingers rise from the newly torn hole, feeling the edges, testing. Soon, it fully emerges and it is clear this is a toddler's arm. It joins the others in wildly moving with no clear pattern or purpose.

"I don't know where it's getting these cells! This new arm is so small...a baby, perhaps 2 years old. Maybe it absorbs and stores them for use later..." the sound of a pencil furiously writing is audible. "Now, I have another test to perform. If you'll just give me a moment!"

The camera is set down near an array of switches and buttons. A man's hand appears and presses them in a deliberate pattern. Finally, he pulls a small lever and a release clicks somewhere in the distance. The camera picks back up and points at the containment cell.

"I had to acquire this test subject quickly, as the nature of the Peeled is so unpredictable. We have no idea how long it will remain in this state. As such, I had to bypass certain...regulations. That's one perk of being the boss, I suppose!" He chuckles and the video focuses on the ceiling of the cell. "Now, let's observe."

A small hatch slides back and a human suspended upside-down is lowered into the cell. He is wearing a straight jacket so that his movement is constricted. He screams and attempts to free himself from the straps, causing his body to swing wildly as it descends into the room. With a jolt, its progress halts. After a moment the man drops to the floor completely, the rope suspending him severed from somewhere above. The hatch closes.

"Please, please, doctor... I don't know what I did, but I promise I can do anything you need..." He is crying and very red in the face. He has made his body rigid and seems to be avoiding any movement now that he is in the room with the Peeled. It can be assumed this creature tracks through vibrations, lacking sight and other senses.

The camera focuses on the man. The doctor coughs, clearing his throat. "You remember my assistant, Henry? Always willing to help, always volunteering for extra duties. This feels perfect for him, doesn't it? To become a permanent part of the study?"

The many arms of the creature clap against the floor of the cell, one after another. Henry screams and crawls away. The slapping becomes frantic, and the Peeled begins to drag itself across the floor with surprising speed, using the arms to lift and move the body. A trail of slime behind it indicates the path taken, similar to a slug.

Henry is still yelling but his voice is becoming hoarse. The Peeled reaches his feet. The hands begin to grab him, climbing up his legs and covering his body with limbs so numerous that soon you cannot see Henry underneath. The Organism shifts, turning. The only visible part of Henry is his head. His mouth opens and closes, but no sound comes from it. One of the appendages breaks free from the pack and approaches. It is the newly birthed child-like limb. Several others pull at Henry's mouth, holding it open. The small fingers disappear down the man's throat. After a few moments, it pulls back, holding what appears to be Henry's organs. With one flourish the rest of them fly out, quickly grabbed by some of the many flailing arms. They crush them between their fingers. Blood, digested food, and other fluids rain down on the Peeled body. It rubs itself, spreading the mess with vigour. Henry's body is discarded into a corner. His chest is concave.

Throughout this, the doctor has remained silent.

"Beautiful," he says and cuts the recording.

Further videotapes were decayed and could not be viewed. Dr. Christensen has not been found.

SEGMENT 15
THE NON-BELIEVER

Never thought my mom would be right. It wasn't how she expected, but near enough that I began to question my life up until that point. I grew up under her well-manicured fist and got out as soon as I could. Took me a long time to realize how many "quirky childhood incidents" were just abuse until my friends pointed it out to me. We'd be swapping stories and I'd mention if the Christmas presents, we got from relatives weren't "Christian enough" she'd throw them out. Threw out a book Kayla lent me once too. I'd be chuckling to myself, and those friends would look back, horrified and full of pity.

We lived and breathed the Bible. Our Dad had been long gone at this point and I don't blame him. Over the years we heard rumours; that he was a Satanist, an adulterer, a criminal. It didn't matter--Mom said the only man in our lives should be the Lord. She told us we were all His special children but that we had to work hard to earn a place with Him. Turns out this meant doing every chore known to man, twice daily, working to the bone scrubbing grout with a toothbrush. I never felt like I was good enough, worked hard enough or that I prayed enough. I remember crying when she'd read Revelations, knowing I'd be left behind to burn. "Maybe we can find a pastor's son to take pity on you, Abigail." The highest achievement my mother could think of was being thrust upon someone, hoping they could put me in my place since she couldn't. That probably planted the seed of doubt in me, which led me to leave them the first second I could.

Got a bank account and job at sixteen, saved every penny. My first apartment was an air mattress and not much else but that first taste of freedom was so, so good. Those friends I mentioned introduced me to some forums for people like me, who got out of that kind of household. We'd lament our upbringings and turn bad memories into memes. Took a long time but things are better now.

Then I got a call that Mom was dying of cancer, wanted to see me. Guess karma finally caught up with her. My sisters barely left her side and then I walked in, blue hair and covered in piercings. They left me to say my goodbyes but in reality, I think they just didn't want to be in the same room as me. Mom said she wanted to tell me something then reached out from her hospital bed and took both my hands in hers.

I saw a scared, frail woman looking back at me. The red-hot rage that terrified my younger self had faded over the years, leaving nothing but embers and ashes. Her knuckles stood out like gnarled roots, her skin like wax paper. This was the person that destroyed me, year after year? Who'd caused so much pain? She was barely more than a whisper. I thought about how little effort it would take to crush her bones, how if I squeezed her neck hard enough, I could pop those eyes right out of her skull.

With all the strength she could muster, my mom told me that the rapture was coming, and God was taking her home. That she tried her best with me, but the fires of Hell were on their way. Maybe, she said, if I begged God's forgiveness for my sins, He would take pity on me. I smiled and nodded but my insides curled up and any love I still held for her dissolved into nothing. When she fell asleep, I left and never returned. A week later she was gone.

When I received an invitation to the funeral (imagine that, being cordially invited to your own mother's funeral) I tore it up directly into the trash and hoped that'd be the end of it.

Two weeks after that, the news started talking about these weird "spots" appearing in several countries. I shrugged it off at first because with the world being as big as it is, weird shit happens every day. Earthquakes, tornadoes, fires…So many disasters Mom would interpret at God's divine judgement. The only difference between a blessing and a curse is which side of the road you're on.

A mining town in Peru reported that instead of copper, they were digging up spongey, red moss. Gunked up the equipment and stalled work for weeks. Scientists who tested the stuff said it was a new kind of lichen, probably unearthed from years of digging, nothing to worry about. When you dig into the Earth for long enough, you're bound to find organisms living in extreme conditions. I remember a colony of fish in the Arctic, untouched for centuries. How strange that must be, to have your entire existence thrust into a larger scale like that.

More and more people flocked to the mine, expressing interest in the potential pharmaceutical benefits of the red moss. The cells did not age, they said. The natural elasticity and fast growth cycle could have incredible industrial potential, said another. The rotting smell could be dealt with, proclaimed a perfume company, and could become a humane alternative to ambergris. The Miracle Moss.

Then a package arrived. Neatly folded brown paper and equally trim handwriting. The kind of wrapping that feels shameful to tear into. Instead, I cut the tape and carefully removed the box inside. It contained two items: a letter, and a small, thick book with a dark red cover. It looked several hundred years old, but in surprisingly good condition. I looked for a title, but it only had two circles, like the number eight. I put it aside and opened the letter.

Dearest Abigail,

I am almost certain you do not remember me, and I sincerely apologize for any difficulties my absence may have caused. You may find this hard to believe, but I did not want to leave your mother. However, our religious differences made it so a compromise was impossible. She believed her way was the right way, as I know mine to be the truth. Any attempt to raise you and your sisters with an equal understanding of scripture ended in screaming. Then, in an unfortunate turn of events and with the help of her connections within the church, I was essentially cast out, both as your father and a member of the community. If you are reading this, then Joyce has passed away. I give you my deepest condolences. I offer you now what I could not give you as a child: the true story of God.

May we become One.

Your loving Father.

I couldn't believe this. All my life I'd been led to believe he left willingly, that he was a no-good heathen. I just sat there for a while processing. Then I flipped open the book. The inside cover had no publisher or other identifying information.

A simple "Dean" was inscribed on the upper corner, matching the writing in the letter. Was that my father's name? I guess so. I rubbed my thumb over the letters absentmindedly. "Oh, shit!" The ink smudged, leaving a smear both on the book and my thumb. A fucking family heirloom and I wrecked it already. Typical. My body heat must have warned it up. I brought my fingers to my face to get a closer look and kneaded it together over my first two fingers. A light, honeylike scent filled my sinuses as the ink became powdery, a tiny cloud of dust before dissipating. "Oh well. Guess it came out easily." I think it got in my nose because I felt a tickle that made me sneeze.

The title on the inside cover brought my attention back to the book. Large, blocky letters that read:

THE DIVINE FLESH OF OUR HOLY FATHER

Pertaining to the events of the Birth of the Universe and what came after.

Translated from original texts, containing the word of the Lord and preparations for His return.

May we become One.

I've never seen something so familiar, yet so strange. It was like having a picture on the wall of your childhood home, and finally, unable to resist, taking it down and peering at the back of the frame. I felt invigorated, my body tingling.

In the beginning, there was only God. From nothing, He created the universe. With every new star, each more magnificent than the one before, a sadness grew in his heart. He had no one to share the joy of life with, utterly alone in the vastness of space.

So, God moulded two children: Solis, the shining star, forever burning bright; and Soma, the glowing beauty, piercing the veil of night. He gave each dominion over the passage of time, to bring forward each day. He watched over his kin and welled with pride as life grew from their love. Then, feeling satisfied with their rule, God returned to the act of creation, content to preside from afar.

But Solis and Soma felt they deserved more. They fought bitterly over who was better, as each desired to govern completely. Each day they battled, and when Soma tired, the day prevailed. When Solis collapsed from pain, the night rang true. This continued for eons, as God continued to expand the cosmos unawares.

Finally satisfied with his work, God returned to greet his children with open arms and was met with claws and fangs, the anger of battle, the pain of loss and the bitterness of time. They began ravaging his immortal flesh. God wept as His flesh was flayed from his bones, becoming the lands. His tears rained down and filled the oceans, the blood splashing created lakes and streams. His bones, crushed into shifting desert sands, His hairs the grasses and trees, His muscles the beasts, and as His heart broke, Man sprung forth.

When their Father was no more, Solis and Soma came to their senses. Overcome with grief the two vowed to never quarrel again, and each has remained in their rightful place to this day. We mourn for the death of God, but we also celebrate, for in dying He brought life to our world. He is here, all around us, and in all of us. Every time you feel a surge of love, that is God speaking through you. When we perish, our bodies rejoin the collective. All life came from Him, and all life will return to Him. And when the pain of his children's betrayal fades, when the strength of His flesh returns, He will rise up and we will become One.

She was wrong. All this time, I felt like I wasn't good enough for God. What kind of all-loving creator would cast people out so easily? The truth was that He didn't care about the borders or precepts that divided men over the millennia. Mom always talked about how going to Heaven is like coming home–but we're already home.

My thoughts felt clear. Like a whale finally set free from a snagging net, boundless energy filled my veins and I set about doing as much research as I could. Websites with scripture and theory. YouTube channels dedicated to undoing the "lies of modern religion".

"The Eucharist," said one vlogger, standing in front of a wooden infinity icon, "is a perversion of the original message. We are not symbolically consuming God--We are a literal part of God. We bleed His blood! When we die, our flesh returns to Him."

He went on to explain how embalming fluids, heavy caskets and cremation prevent the merging effectively. "Some cultures, who perform sky burials or natural decomposition, are closer to the original message. Death is not the end, it's a set towards restoration."

It only took me a few days to make a decision. The drive to the city was peaceful, and I switched on the radio. "The time has come!" A powerful, determined voice crackled as I found the right station. "After all these years He has finally been brought back. Seek solace, my brothers and sisters, as we will be together soon. Seek out the clusters!"

As I drove, more and more people were headed in the same direction. It was calling us home. Cutting the engine, I saw The Pile: a writhing mass of bodies climbing into the sky. Some were singing, some crying. It was beautiful. I could barely contain my excitement as I joined them.

REINTEGRATION

"Welcome back to CKWB, your source for news in the Whittaker Valley. This is In The Know, where we discuss current events affecting our community and the world at large. I'm Rebecca Bain, and sitting with me today is Dr. Laurie Forrester, the world's foremost expert on the phenomena known as the Outers. After the so-called 'Event,' our world changed forever, and society is still picking up the pieces. Dr. Forrester is the head of the Reintegration project, researching ways to bring people back from the Outer infection as well as the origins of the outbreak so that it never happens again. Tell me doctor, what is your opinion on the Anti-Integration protests? That we eradicate the remaining Outers?"

Laurie sits straight and tries to summon all the air of intelligence her position requires her to have. She'd worn the best navy pantsuit she owned and let her hair down for once, her soft brunette waves sitting around her shoulders. Rebecca was the best daytime host around and Laurie felt shabby in comparison. The In The Know set with its artificial friendliness felt like a relic of the past, before millions had died or turned to paste. A silver ring on a chain tinkles against her throat as she answers:

"Well, Rebecca, that's a good question. I understand their anger and grief over losing loved ones--I lost my wife and son during the crisis--but these are still human beings who deserve respect and consideration just like everyone else. That's why it's important that our research--"

Rebecca put her hand up. "I'm sorry to interrupt Dr. Forrester, but are you saying we should forgive those who killed and cannibalised our friends and loved ones?"

Laurie took a quick, deep breath: "I did not say that. Forgiveness is a personal matter. You have to remember this is a disease–these people didn't intend to kill anyone. Their brains were in literal overdrive and most of our patients have little to no memories of their sickness. What I mean to say is that to truly move on from this–and get back to 'normal'-- we must proceed with Reintegration no matter how uncomfortable it makes some of us." The more she spoke, the more she started to believe in it herself. "Our research on separating each individual from within a cluster is progressing at a steady pace and we are confident that reuniting with loved ones is indeed a possibility."

"I assume you're talking about the Artificial Derma Project?"

"Yes. Early test results have been very promising." Laurie turns and addresses the camera directly. "I should mention we are seeking able-bodied volunteers for this. You will be doing your country a great service and your family will be well provided for." Turning back to her interviewer, Laurie's voice becomes more casual.

"In fact, Rebecca, one of the reasons I'm here today is to unveil our latest model, which we are calling Derma V3.0. Alex, would you come out here please?"

Laurie stood up and stepped down from the living room set to the open stage area of the studio. From behind a curtain, a large, cylindrical tank on wheels approached slowly. The tank was mounted on a small platform with many wires and indicators going in and out of the container. The movements were stunted and robotic, and no operator was visible. She leaned down and flipped a switch, making the opaque tank crystal clear.

Inside was a tangled mess of tubes and lumps. It wiggled in response to the bright studio lights now aimed at it. The mass resembled a jellyfish, a bloblike, top-heavy clump of tissue that sat atop spaghetti thin wires and tubes, feeding nutrients and removing waste. The liquid it was suspended in was murky, with dark spots floating around the main body. As it moved, those spots swirled. Layers of similarly dark sediment sat at the base, creating a morbid aquarium. A single eyeball sat directly on the pile. It darted around, taking in its surroundings and came to rest on Laurie, who had placed her palm flat on the tank.

"As I mentioned, I lost my wife. That is true. But the conditions of her infection were not as severe as others, and we had the advantage of facilities where we could keep her safe until a cure was found." Laurie smiled and ran her hand along the glass surface, gazing at the remains of her spouse, now nothing more than an oversized wad of gum.

She switched back to presentation mode in an instant. "As you can see, the newest technology in artificial bodies has advanced leaps and bounds--thanks to the funding provided by MR&C--between version 2.0 and 3.0. We've made this one clear as an example, so you can see all of the salvaged organs; the stomach, pancreas, and intestines are all present and the partial brain stem works in conjunction with the power supply." She pointed to each body part as she listed them off. "It runs on a self-contained nuclear core that is perfectly safe. The ADP fluid keeps all organic material in a stable environment and recycles all waste products, if applicable."

"PppleeeAAAse...........LET ME oooOUUT..." A flurry of bubbles rose from the creature as it strained to communicate, and it began to sway back and forth in the limited space it occupied.

"Did you hear that, doctor? Did it speak?" Rebecca was standing up now, backing away and desperately glancing in the direction of the cameraman and producers who were now aimed at her.

"Oh, no, no, no. You must be hearing feedback from my microphone. This model does have vocal functionality, but it's been switched off to not interfere with this interview." Laurie crouched down and fiddled with various buttons, frowning.

"Oh, umm. Wait--something's happening! Doctor, what's going on? Is this part of the demonstra--what is it doing?!"

The camera panned from Rebecca's shocked face back to the tank. The thing that was once Alex slammed against the glass container as Laurie held it up, bracing herself with one knee on the floor. With a yelp, she slipped. The machine fell on top of the doctor, crushing her instantly. Blood and fluid spread quickly on the floor. The glass was shattered.

"Oh, my God. Ohhh, my God. Tony, make sure you're zooming in." She'd stepped out of the set completely now, but was stabbing a finger in the direction of the action.

The Alex-thing slid out of the jagged hole, ripping itself in the process. It clenched and unclenched, propelling itself closer to Laurie's half-crushed head like a worm. The machine had pushed innards out of her chest like toothpaste. Sliding over the dead woman's face, the mass shuddered. Tony lifted the camera from the tripod and moved around the stage in a half-circle to get a better view. Bit by bit, Alex was growing smaller until it disappeared completely down Laurie's throat. Her body began convulsing violently and slid out from under the tank, separating from the crunched flesh and bones. With a snap, the arms twisted backwards, lifting off the ground with great effort. Lumbering towards Tony.

"Keep filming! Keep filming!" Rebecca had come up behind him, screaming in his ear. Her presence threw Tony off balance, and he tripped over a cord. He and his camera smashed on to the hard floor, still facing the creature.

As if curious at the turn of events, it stopped, cocking its head from side to side like a dog trying to listen. One eye blinked, then the other. Laurie's face, dripping gore and mucus, smiled. "It'SSSss OK now. W'e'RE ToGETHerr AgAAin."

84

AFTERWORD

When I was around 13, I was obsessed with becoming a writer. It was my first real dream, something that actually existed (in contrast to my earlier dream of becoming a Pokémon Trainer). I bought fancy filigree journals with the intention of writing a story from start to finish, a physical book I could share with people. I do not recommend this. My handwriting is sloppy and I wrote it in pen. It was around this time that my mental illness came into full swing and my creative energy in all mediums dissipated. I spent years trying to figure out who I was and what I wanted to do. I never felt good enough. It's only because of the terrible state of the world in late 2020, that a switch flipped in my brain: Why not? What's the worst that could happen? So, I began writing about horror, and soon realized it was actually something I could do. I enjoyed writing, researching, and putting myself out there to interact with the horror community at large, who are some of the nicest people I've ever known. I feel like I have finally found my place in this world.

It will sound very cliché, but the central ideas for Inside Out came to me in a dream. I was in the role of Jake, feeling my eyes burn away as I dissolved. It's quite a rarity for me to remember my dreams, but this one felt so vivid. I began to write it down and expand on a central idea; how would people of different backgrounds, ages, and other factors deal with these creatures? I wanted to explore every aspect of the body and how gross that can get! Huge thanks and appreciation to my friends Bear, Tig, Spooky, Uber, George, and Sy for their support and for putting up with me when I would ask them their opinions on the grossness factor. Apologies to people I borrowed names from, especially my high school Japanese teacher Mr. Christensen, who was the nicest person in the world and not at all like my version. In memory of my biggest creative inspiration, Kentaro Miura, author of Berserk who sadly passed away in May of 2021. To the Horror Obsessive crew: Robin, Emma, and especially Andrew and Rebecca for giving this newbie a chance. My editor, Matt; your kindness and work has made this book the best it can be. Thank you to Shanelle, my cheerleader and constant supporter. Finally, to my partner, thank you for your love, your patience, and always knowing how to make me laugh.

* * * * *

This book was written on Treaty 8 Territory, the ancestral and traditional land of the Cree, Dene, and Métis people. I am grateful for the Traditional Knowledge Keepers and Elders who are with us today and those who have come before, living and caring for these lands for generations. Indigenous people are treated as if the systemic violence they experience is a thing of the past. Missing and murdered indigenous women and residential school survivors, and the thousands who did not survive, are proof enough that these issues are a daily reality. We must acknowledge the harm settler institutions continue to perpetuate against Indigenous Peoples and do what we can to dismantle these systems of oppression.

A Note From DarkLit Press

All of us at DarkLit Press want to thank you for taking the time to read this book. Words cannot describe how grateful we are knowing that you spent your valuable time and hard-earned money on our publication. We appreciate any and all feedback from readers, good or bad. Reviews are extremely helpful for indie authors and small businesses (like us). We hope you'll take a moment to share your thoughts on Amazon, Goodreads and/or BookBub.

You can also find us on all the major social platforms including Facebook, Instagram, and Twitter. Our horror community newsletter comes jam-packed with giveaways, free or deeply discounted books, deals on apparel, writing opportunities, and insights from genre enthusiasts.

LoR Gislason

Lor Gislason (they/them) is an autistic non-binary homebody from Vancouver Island, Canada. Their articles have been featured on Hear Us Scream, Horror Obsessive and several upcoming anthologies. Their dream is to one day make an encyclopedia covering body horror films.

Follow Lor on Twitter @lorelli_

Content Warnings

Body Horror
Viral Infections, Pandemics
Cannibalism
Animal Dissection
Child Death, Parent Death
Vomit
Mentions of Animal, Spousal, Child, and Elder Abuse
Marijuana Mention
Masturbation and Fellatio
Self-Harm/Skin Picking
Transphobia
Gun Violence
Human Liquification
Rotting Food/Eating Rotting Food
Alcohol
Surgery Mention
Scientific Experimentation/Torture
Human Sacrifice
Religion
Cancer
Natural Disasters
Implied Suicide

DARKLIT
PRESS